Dinosaur Chase

Dinosaur

by Carolyn Otto

Chase

illustrated by Thacher Hurd

HarperCollins Publishers

The hand lettering is by Donna Allman.

The pictures of the rocket ship and the baseball player on page 31 are by Nicholas Hurd.

The artwork was painted with india ink and transparent watercolors.

Dinosaur Chase
Text copyright © 1991 by Carolyn B. Otto
Illustrations copyright © 1991 by Thacher Hurd
Printed in the U.S.A. All rights reserved.
1 2 3 4 5 6 7 8 9 10
First Edition

Library of Congress Cataloging-in-Publication Data
Otto, Carolyn.
    Dinosaur chase / by Carolyn Otto ; illustrated by Thacher Hurd.
        p.   cm.
    Summary: A mother dinosaur reads her sleepy dinosaur son a bedtime
story about a dinosaur chase that occurs when a precious necklace is
stolen.
    ISBN 0-06-021613-1. — ISBN 0-06-021614-X (lib. bdg.)
    [1. Dinosaurs—Fiction.   2. Bedtime—Fiction.]   I. Hurd, Thacher,
ill.   II. Title.
PZ7.08794Di   1991   90-2021
[E]—dc20   CIP
                                                                          AC

For KZ and PDH
C.B.O.

For Marilyn Marlow
T.H.

dinosaur two legs

dinosaur four

dinosaur swim

swish swish

dinosaur fishing

for dinosaur fish

tiptoe dinosaur

dinosaur sneak

run run
dinosaur run

hiding in

a dinosaur place

dinosaur snore